The Boy
Who Made
Dragonfly

The Boy
Who Made
Dragonfly

A Zuni Myth

Retold by Tony Hillerman

Illustrated by Laszlo Kubinyi

Harper & Row, Publishers
New York, Evanston, San Francisco, London

*For Anne, Jan, Tony, Monica, Steve,
and Dan—and all other children
(and former children) who have
time to listen.*

The author wishes to acknowledge the valuable advice and assistance of Joe Shaw, a good friend who understands what words are all about.

The Boy
Who Made
Dragonfly

1

It happened before the A'shiwi, the Flesh of the Flesh, finally found the Middle Place and ended their long wanderings. It happened before the A'shiwi came to be called the Zunis, before the Water Strider stretched his arms and legs to the edges of the world and lowered his body to the place where the A'shiwi were to live. It happened when the people still lived in the Valley of Hot Waters in the good stone town they called Ha'wi-k'uh. It happened long before the white man came.

In those days the A'shiwi had been given by the Beloved Ones an abundance of water blessings.

In the Valley of Hot Waters, there was a richness of rain. The mud washed down the arroyos and the A'shiwi spread it across their flatlands with dams of brush. It was that way year after year. And in the winter, the Ice God rarely blew his breath toward them because two of the Corn Maidens lived just south of there and looked after the people-who-would-be-called Zunis. Summer after summer, the A'shiwi grew more corn than they could eat. The storerooms of all the women were filled to the rafters and all the A'shiwi were as fat as October gophers.

One day in the autumn, when the people had brought in their corn, they had so much that they would have to build new storerooms and they piled it in the plaza. The Chief Priest of the Bow was standing on top of his house looking down at this great wealth of corn. As he looked, his mind became swollen with pride in his people. None other of all the tribes around the Middle Place had accumulated such an abundance that their storerooms overflowed. While he was thinking about this, and what he should tell the A'shiwi to do with this richness of seed food, he noticed some children playing at war. They were throwing balls of mud at each other, and as he watched their game, this Priest of the Bow, this member of the great Bow Society, this valuable man of the village, began to think as a little child thinks before he learns how to live. The Priest of the Bow thought that it would be good to let the Navajos and the Utes and the Lagunas and the Acomas and the Hopis and all the other nations know how rich the A'shiwi had become.

The Bow Priest called together the valuable men of all the clans, and the Pekwin, and the six A'shi-wa-ni priests, and the leaders of the kiva societies, and the Mudheads, and everyone else who was the most valuable. When they were in council, he spoke to them.

"Listen," he said. "I think it would be a good thing for the A'shiwi if we showed all the other people how rich we have become. I think it would be a good thing if we had all our people prepare a great feast. It would be good if we had the women bake a great store of hard bread and soft bread, corn cakes, tortillas, and other things, and make a great supply of sweet mush and all other foods. Then it would be good if we sent out our fast-running young men to summon all the other nations to come to Ha'wi-k'uh to join us in celebrating our water blessings. We will have all who come join us in a great battle, such as the children play, and we will use bread, and mush dough, and foodstuffs for our weapons. Valuable men, think on this! Think of how these strangers will marvel at the wealth of the A'shiwi, when they see us treating the food for which others labor so hard as the children treat the mud by the riverside and the stones of the mesas."

The other valuable men were just as foolish as the Bow Priest. *"Ha'tchi!"* they all said. "You have thought well, and spoken well. Let it be done as you say."

And so the village of Ha'wi-k'uh became loud with sounds. There was the noise of the men breaking the wood to fit into the ovens, and the noise of the metates grinding mountains of yellow corn, and the roar of the fires in the *hornos* where the food was baking. And the village was covered with a cloud of piñon smoke from the ovens and the steam from the boiling pots of mush. And while this was happening, the runners went out in all the directions to tell the other nations.

Now the Corn Maidens heard of what the people of Ha'wi-k'uh were doing. It made them sad that their children would waste the food of the water blessing. But the White Corn Maiden said that perhaps it was not as they heard it was. And the Yellow Corn Maiden said that perhaps the people of Ha'wi-k'uh were seeking a way to share

So the Corn Maidens came in and the old woman took off her ragged blanket and spread it on the floor for them to sit upon. She put the cornmeal she had boiled for her own supper into a bowl for them and worked straightening out things around the room—the way women do—so her guests wouldn't notice there was nothing for her to eat. But the Yellow Corn Maidens noticed anyway.

"An old mother as kind and gentle as you should not go without your supper," the Yellow Corn Maiden said. "Sit happy here and join us at this meal because we, too, have some food."

Then the White Corn Maiden brought from under her torn blanket a pouch made of buckskin and beaded with turquoise and the whitest shells. From that, she took out honeycomb, corn cakes, and the bread that is made with meal and piñon nuts. Then she took out a pouch of pollen and sprinkled it over the old woman's lumpy cornmeal mush. A mist rose up from the pot and it smelled like a meadow of spring flowers. And when the old mother saw this happen, she knew that these poor women must be two of the Corn Maidens, or two of the other Beloved Ones who A'wonawil'ona made to help look after the A'shiwi. The old mother felt ashamed that she had

11

been so bold as to invite the Beloved Ones into her broken old house. She huddled over by the wall away from them.

Then the Yellow Corn Maiden spoke to her. "Old mother, know now who we are and know why we come here. We are Yellow Corn Maiden and White Corn Maiden, and we come to look at our children, the A'shiwi, the Flesh of the Flesh. But now we find that you and two little ones up in the village must be the only true A'shiwi who are left in Ha'wi-k'uh. So come, sit happy with us and be satisfied. You asked us to eat with you. We ask you now to eat with us."

The old mother was still afraid but she got out her prayer meal and sprinkled it on the heads of the Corn Maidens, blessing them. And as she sat to eat with them, she saw their hair was no longer grizzled white with age, but black and glossy with youth, and their wrists jangled with perfect silver, and their faces were beautiful with happiness. The old mother dipped her fingers into the coarse corn mush and found it had become sweet and rich to taste, as if it had been mixed with honey. And the Corn Maidens talked to her and laughed and made jokes. The old mother's lonely old heart forgot its years of solitude and remembered how it had been when her sons had been around her and her house had been full of the sounds of children.

When they had all satisfied themselves, the White Corn Maiden brought out a bundle and unrolled it on the floor. Inside was a white cape of fringed doeskin. "Hang this on your blanket pole, kind mother," the White Corn Maiden said, "and on the morning after you hang it there, you will find under it meal, and melons, and all good things to eat, in plenty. We leave you this because our water blessing will no longer come to Ha'wi-k'uh." By then Sun-Father had left the sky and gone to his sacred place, and darkness covered Corn Mountain, and the Corn Maidens breathed on the hands of the old mother, and she breathed on their hands, and they went away.

When the last knot in the calendar cord was untied and the day for the great festival came, the people of Ha'wi-k'uh put on their finest silver and turquoise and their strings of whitest shell and the best of their blankets and the softest deerskin. As Sun-Father came standing out from his sacred place, the pathways to the pueblo were covered in all directions with the strangers coming in, as bidden by the A'shiwi runners. The housetops of the village were covered with breadstuffs, with hard cakes and soft, and with great pots of batter and meal. As the morning passed, the priests of the Bow Society began dividing up the clans into armies for the great war game. The Badger Clan

would be on this side, and the Turkey Clan on that, the Yellow-wood Clan on this, and the To-bacco Clan on that. And when the Sun-Father had reached his highest point in the sky for that day, the mock battle began.

The air over the pueblo of Ha'wi-k'uh at that moment was filled with flying bread, and blobs of boiled mush, and all other food. Some warriors were knocked to the earth by hard bread, and some were splattered across their faces with dough, and everyone's hair and robes were smeared with corn-meal batter. The A'shiwi shrieked with laughter

and the visiting strangers smiled a little, but mostly they talked quietly among themselves—trying to think of the reasons the A'shiwi behaved in this way. The girls were standing on the rooftops, laughing and throwing hard bread down at the young men fighting below. As it is when young men are being looked upon by maidens, the warriors began to fight harder with one another, and to get angry, and to cause pain. By the time darkness finally came, almost everybody in the pueblo was angry and disgusted and soon the moon rose over a town that was sullen with silence.

When dawn came and the people climbed out of their roofs to make their prayer to the Sun-Father, they were astonished by what they saw. A murmur of surprise and worry could be heard all across the village. The great plaza of Ha'wi-k'uh had been covered the night before with the breadstuffs used in the great war game, but now in the light of the dawn the people saw that it had been swept clean. The A'shiwi were disturbed by this—some because they had planned to gather in the food they had thrown (after the strangers had gone and could not see them do it) to save it for the winter, and some because it seemed strange and unnatural that all the foodstuffs would thus vanish during the night. They soon understood that the seed-eaters had taken it, because all around the pueblo they found the tracks of the animals. But even this seemed unnatural. How had the seed-eaters known to come?

Even so, they said to each other: "What matters it? Be happy. Our storerooms still hold enough corn to last us through the winter. And when summer comes again, there will be another harvest of great bounty."

For the old mother in the broken house below the village, the view at dawn caused great dismay. She had gone to her bed the night before thinking that when morning came the people of Ha'wi-k'uh would throw the breadstuffs they had used in their war game down around her hut as they always threw their trash. She awoke that morning happy, thinking to go out from her house and gather in this wasted food and thus have something to keep her old body alive through the winter. But alas! When she climbed through her roof hole and looked about her, she saw there was no wasted food —the village had been picked as clean as an old bone. She climbed back down the ladder, thinking to make herself a breakfast of her rough ground meal. But as she did, she remembered the robe the Corn Maidens had left for her—and the magic they had told her the robe would work. She went into the room where she had hung the robe on the blanket pole. Lo! In that room, under this robe, the old mother saw a sight to startle her eyes. Against the walls were stacked cords of white corn, and yellow corn, and corn of mixed colors. And around it were baskets of squash, and melons, and dried fruits, and piñon nuts, and jerked venison.

When she saw these things, tears came to the eyes of the old woman and a great weight lifted from her heart. Because, now, the winter held no fear. She would survive the days and nights of cold. But there was also a sadness in her thoughts. She longed for a chance to tell the Corn Maidens of the peace they had brought to her. But she longed even more for someone to tell of her good fortune —and to share it with her.

2

Time and winter passed and then came the winds of spring. But this year the winds blew steadily from the west. Never did they blow with the water blessing from the Rain God of the South, and no rains came to make the flatlands of Ha'wi-k'uh ready for the corn seeds. The people of Ha'wi-k'uh were troubled by this. But they planted even more of their supply of corn seed than they usually would, because they wished to repeat their war-game-with-food festival when the harvest came. The corn sprouted weak and yellow from the dry-ness of its roots. The A'shiwi planted prayer

19

plumes of the most beautiful feathers, and sang the proper prayers most carefully, and performed the most valuable dances, with every word sung and every step done exactly in the proper fashion. But the water blessing did not come. Each afternoon, the clouds would climb the sky from the horizon. But as the prayers of the A'shiwi drew them toward the cornfields of Ha'wi-k'uh, the monster called Cloud-Swallower would rise into the sky and drink them all down. Day after day through the hot summer this would happen. The priests and valuable men of the kiva fraternities would perform their most precious dances, and bury prayer plumes made in the most valuable way, and the clouds would be drawn toward the cornfields. And then Cloud-Swallower would arise, invisible to the A'shiwi, and suck down all the mist and vapor, so no rain could fall. The corn yellowed. The corn died, its dead stalks brittle in the fields.

Many weeks earlier, the people of Ha'wi-k'uh had stopped talking of holding another war game and began talking only of whether there would be enough to eat. Now they felt despair. As winter came again, the A'shiwi roamed the mesas collecting the dried fruits of the cactus, and the roots of plants that can be eaten, and the nuts of the piñons. But the failure of the water blessing had left even these poor foodstuffs scarce in the country-side. The mule deer had moved northward where the springs still ran and the browse was better, and even the rabbits and the prairie dogs had left the drought-stricken countryside.

By the time of the days of the longest darkness, in the dead, cold heart of winter, the last of the corn from the storerooms had been ground and eaten. The people then were pitifully poor. The children sorted through the dust in search for stray kernels that might have fallen from the cobs, and the men hunted through the snowy mesas for game which would no longer be lured by their hunting chants. The buckskin of their robes was toasted, old bones were ground for food on the meal stones, and everywhere there was hunger.

From her broken house below the village, the old mother saw the misery of her people and wished to help. But when the A'shiwi saw the woman of the broken house was no thinner than she had ever been and had food when they had none, they concluded that she had joined the brotherhood of sorcerers. Thus, when the old woman offered food, in her kindness, they were afraid to take it. Each of them knew in his heart that he had treated the old mother cruelly. Each presumed that she now sought her revenge as a sorceress. So it happened that only the birds and the hungry animals of the village shared in the blessings given the old woman by the Corn Maidens.

In the darkest days of winter, the very old and the very young among the A'shiwi began to weaken from hunger, and to sicken, and to die. A council was called of all the kivas and the fraternities and the clans. The priests and the valuable men each spoke their thoughts. And when the council ended, it was decided that if the people were to survive they must abandon Ha'wi-k'uh and find food. The Council sent runners westward to the villages of the Hopis to ask if they could feed the A'shiwi until the spring. After many days had passed, two young messengers from the Hopis arrived at Ha'wi-k'uh bearing lengths of knotted cord numbering the days until the Hopis would be prepared to greet and feed the A'shiwi.

There was great excitement among the houses of Ha'wi-k'uh then. To reach the Hopi villages they must walk many days across the broken lands covered with snow and barren of food. Would they have enough food to keep them alive on this bitter journey? Perhaps, the priests decided, but only if they left that very night—before more of their pitiful supply was eaten.

That night there was much haste. In all the houses of Ha'wi-k'uh the people worked through the dark hours gathering what leather and bone meal could be found, searching everywhere for anything that could be eaten to keep them alive. Long before morning, the call went out from the rooftops of the village that all was ready and that the sturdy young runners from the Hopi villages were leaving to lead the A'shiwi. When the people heard this call, they rushed from their houses. They were terrified that, weak as they were from hunger, they would be left behind by the strong young strangers.

Now it happened that in the house of the boy and girl who had offered bread to the Corn Maidens, there lived an old uncle who had good reason for such fear. This man had been a Koyemshi, one of the wisest of the wise fraternity of Mudhead Clowns. But now he was the oldest man of Ha'wi-k'uh, too weak to wear the mask of mud and do the hard work of the brotherhood of clowns. He had the hardihood of the aged and the walk through the snow to the Hopi villages held no fear for him. But his legs hobbled only slowly. This old uncle had already earned the anger of many of the villagers. He had warned the valuable men of the kivas, before the great war games, that treating foodstuffs as children treat the river mud was not the way of the A'shiwi. He had chided the people for failing to feed the ragged beggar women. And, when the priests and their student priests vainly danced their most sacred rituals to draw the blessed clouds over the dying corn, he had told the A'shiwi that their own foolishness had caused this great trouble. That had angered the village, and he wished not to anger his people again by lagging behind. So this old uncle left early, knowing the villagers would soon overtake him.

The boy and the girl had worked late helping prepare for the trip, but finally they had fallen asleep in a warm corner beside the hearth. When the voice of the Pekwin sounded over the village, urging all forth to follow the Hopi guides, there was a rush in this house for the ladders to the roof holes, and in this rush the two little ones were forgotten. It was only when the night was gone and the villagers had struggled many miles past the Zuni buttes that their parents realized they were not with the column. And then it was thought that perhaps they had gone ahead with the old uncle. If not, their path was certainly completed.

By then it was clear that this journey would be very hard, few of the little ones would survive, and those who straggled behind would surely die. It was better to let them sleep. If someone went back for them now, neither he nor the children would ever catch up again.

The brother and his little sister slept peacefully. The Sun-Father emerged from his sacred place and lit the eastern sky, but still they slept because they were both tired from their labors and weak from the long hunger, and because the village was drained now of all other life and was as silent as the snow. When the little boy finally awoke, he looked around the great room of his house, saw that it was empty and silent, and realized at once what had happened.

A great fear overcame him for a moment, and tears welled from his eyes. But then he thought of his little sister. He must somehow keep her from fear and harm.

The boy built a fire of bark and piñon sticks in the hearth to warm the room, and then he scrambled up the ladder through the roof hole. It was just as he had guessed. All around him, the village of Ha'wi·k'uh lay silent and empty. No smoke rose from the roof holes of any of the houses. The boy would have cried again in his hunger and his loneliness, but just then he heard his sister awakening. The little girl cried out for mush (of which, maybe, she had been dreaming) so the boy climbed down the ladder and looked everywhere he could think of for something to cook for her.

Alas, there was nothing. But then the boy remembered that from the rooftop, he had seen a flight of birds in the air below the village. And he remembered that he had been told how to catch birds.

He pulled from his head some of the long hairs. These he tied carefully into slip nooses and arranged them neatly over cedar and piñon twigs from the pile of firewood. And then he tied rags around his feet to protect them from the snow (his moccasins had long since been parched and eaten) and went out to set his snares.

The boy noticed hundreds of wrens, and sparrows, and snowbirds, and even piñon jays clustered around the broken house under the village where the old mother lived. But the boy knew that the villagers had avoided this house, and had kept away from the old mother who lived there. He thought she would be gone, now, with the other villagers. But perhaps she had been a sorceress. It would be best to avoid a house where sorcery had been practiced. The boy did not know the birds were attracted there, because, early each morning, the old mother fed them from her doorway. He thought they might be some magical lure of witchcraft. And so it happened that as the winter grew in cold and darkness, neither the boy nor the old mother knew the other was in the village. The old woman, whose ancient bones were quick to chill, stayed inside her broken house, and the boy kept to the other side of the village. There he set out his twigs, with the nooses attached, and hid himself away. Within the hour, three birds had caught themselves. The boy gathered them in and skinned them and took them home to his sister. When he had spitted them and roasted them over the coals, he gently awoke the child.

27

At first she cried for parched corn. And then she noticed there were no old ones around the house and she cried for her mother. But the boy finally got her to drink water and to satisfy herself with the roasted birds.

Thus the two little ones lived, day after day. But the little sister grew sadder and sadder, wishing for seed food, and parched corn, and breadstuffs. She tired of eating nothing but the winter birds and longed for the food to which she was accustomed. More and more, she cried, and the boy found it more and more difficult to comfort her.

Thus it happened that one day he said:

"Hush, little sister. Hush your crying. If you will smile again I will get you something pretty with which to play. I will get you whatever would please your heart."

On hearing this the little girl stopped her crying and thought. And after she had thought for a moment, she told her brother that her sadness would end if he would bring her a butterfly. She said this, probably, because she was weary of the hunger and cold of the winter and the butterfly is the insect of warmth and summer, the time of green corn, and fruit, and squash. Whatever the reason she said it, the words at first brought despair to the mind of her brother. He climbed to the roof hole and looked around. Everywhere the landscape was the black and gray and white of winter. The first butterfly would be months away. As he looked across the cornfields where the insects flew in the summer, a thought came to him. He would make a butterfly.

The boy hurried to the fields and gathered dried stalks of corn and the straw of grasses and with these he hastened home lest his sister would miss him and cry again. He arranged his materials on the blanket beside the child so that she could be amused by his work.

First he built a cage. He cut eight equal sections of cornstalk, and stripped away the hard covering so that only the pith remained. In both ends of each of these eight pieces, he bored holes. Then, using the softer grass as a weaver uses his yarn, he tied the sections together into two square frames. These shaped the top and bottom of his cage. Then he cut stiff straws of grass into identical lengths, and used these as the bars of his cage— sticking their ends into the softness of the pith. Soon the cage was made.

He decorated it with feathers and paints from the boxes of ceremonial things his father and his uncles had left behind. A string of woven hairs

29

served to hang it over the robes where his sister slept, by the hearth.

When his sister had wearied of watching him and had fallen asleep, he began the butterfly. He shaped the body from a long piece of pith, carving the head round and the proper body sections. And then he tried to make the wings. But the biggest pieces of pith he could find were far too narrow, and when he tried to join sections into the shape of wider wings the brittle substance would crumble. Finally the boy knew he could never make the wide wings of the butterfly from the materials at his hands. Instead, he gave the insect two long, narrow wings on each side of its body. And then he gave the fly its six legs, made of bent grass straws. On both sides of the head, he used black paint to form the eyes. But the paint was mixed too thin and the eyes spread much too large for those of a butterfly. He had the same trouble when he tried to paint the spots that give the butterfly wings their color. The red, yellow, blue, and black pigments spread and ran, forming stripes instead of circles. And finally, when the boy was finished and ready to put the paint pots away, the toy looked very little like the butterfly he had promised his sister. Instead he had created a wonderful creature, like none before him had ever

seen. And to this, at the point of balance between its wings, he looped a knotted hair and thus suspended his little effigy from the top of the cage.

When the little girl awoke and saw this being so suspended, just out of reach above her sleeping robes, the sound of her laughter was heard in the house for the first time since the old ones had left them. She wanted, in her joy, to call this bright and graceful being a name. Butterfly was not the right name, that was easy to see, so she called it the words which mean "being-which-flies-on-double-wings." All that day the little one talked to the Cornstalk Being, laughing and chattering and making it swing in its cage. She told her brother that Being-That-Flies lived and understood her words, and the boy's heart was light to see that it made his sister forget her sorrows.

That night before she slept, the pains of her hunger came again to the little one as she played, and she said to Being-That-Flies:

"Fly away to where you can find yellow corn and bring back grains to my brother that he may parch them for my breakfast."

As these words were said, the boy believed, for a moment, that he saw the wings of the Cornstalk Insect flutter with such speed that they blurred before his eyes and hummed like the sound of summer bees. But as he saw this, he knew that the blurring was caused by nothing more than the dizziness of his hunger—that wings made of corn pith do not fly.

The sister, too, thought she had seen the wings flutter. She bounced with joy and laughed. "O, my brother. Did you see that the Being heard my voice and moved his wings?"

"Yes, I saw, little sister. I was afraid he would break out of his cage and fly away," the boy said. He said it only to cheer his sister.

But that night, as the boy lay on his sleeping robes waiting for sleep to take him and watching the light of the stars through the smoke hole, he thought of how it would be if the Corn Being he had made could indeed fly and could somehow find food as his sister had asked. Without it, he feared that the child would not live through the winter. And while he was thinking this, feeling a great longing for some way to help the little one, he heard something like the humming of tiny wings and a whispering sound.

"*Thli-ni-ni*," the whisper said. "Let me go."

The boy lay rigid on his robes, listening.

"Let me go, let me go," whispered the sound.

The boy was so frightened that he could hardly move his tongue. "Where are you?" he said. "Who are you?"

"In this cage," the whisper said.

The boy saw then that the cage with the Corn-stalk Creature was shaking on its string. In the dim light of the stars, he could see it flying against the straw which barred its passage—circling on the thread of hair on which it hung from the cage top.

"Wait, little creature. I will get you water to drink and I will try to find you food, if I but knew what you eat," the boy said. "I would let you go, but if you fly out of our house you will surely die of cold. And if you fly away, my sister will mourn for your going. Therefore you must say to me before I open your cage that you will not fly outside this warm room."

"I do," the Corn Being said. "I say it."

So the boy opened the cage and carefully released the noose of hair which held the Corn-stalk Insect. The little creature flew with marvelous swiftness, darting into all corners of the room. And finally it hovered near the ear of the boy.

"Your heart is greater than the hearts of most of the A'shiwi," the creature said. "You, who have had great reason for anger, have kept anger away from you, and you have loved this poor child, thy sister, faithfully and well." The voice of the insect was a low humming voice and the boy had to strain to hear it, even in the silent night. "You, great-hearted boy, are my father. Because you have given me a body where there was no body before, and twin wings with which I can hover, as no other flying things. And because you made me out of unselfish love you have touched me with life. And I, the product of your mind, am your creature and wish now only to serve you. Release me from my promise. Let me fly through the smoke hole through which the starlight comes. I will return before Sun-Father lights the east. I will spend the night seeking a way to serve you and your sister. But whether or not I fail, I shall return. I will not leave you."

The boy was frightened by this. But he found a tiny pinch of prayer meal and scattered it over the insect in blessing, and told the creature it was free to go.

The insect darted twice around the darkness of the room, with a buzzing hum, and then shot through the smoke hole like an arrow shot by a strong-armed hunter.

The boy lay back on his sleep robes, wondering at what he had seen and heard and if the creature he had made of cornstalk would ever return. And soon sleep took him in.

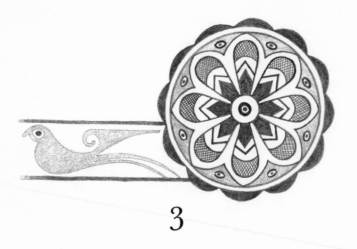

3

The Cornstalk Being soared high over the rooftops of Ha'wi-k'uh, circled higher than the hunting eagle, and finally darted westward. It flew like an arrow across the great mesa and the valleys and the depths of the arroyos and finally it came to the canyons of the Colorado Chiqueto where the water runs roaring red, and at last it hovered over a great blue lake. From where it hovered on its double wings, the insect could see deep into the blue water, see below the surface dim lights as numberless as the winter stars. And on the sandy shores he saw the Water Beings, their ugly bird faces smiling with their kindness, pacing and watching ceaselessly for the souls of men who had fulfilled the pathway of their lives, and who were ready to begin the second life of endless joy. And when the insect saw these things he knew he had found the Sacred Lake. At that moment, he pointed his tail at the sky and his head at the blue shield of water, and dove with the speed of a plummeting falcon. He paused not to speak to the Watcher Beings but sped past them, plunging into the cold, clear water with the sound of an arrow striking.

Almost at once, the Cornstalk Being penetrated the water roof and found himself in a hall blazing with the light of a thousand fires and crowded with happy souls of the Beloved Ones. He was in the Dance Hall of the Dead where the souls of men with their paths fulfilled celebrate their happiness. And at one end, the insect saw the Council of the Gods, with the great Shalako Messenger Birds attending them. He buzzed and darted around the room, resting a moment on a blanket pole here, and on the lip of a pot there, until finally the Little Fire God, Shulawitsi, noticed him.

"Look, my uncles," Shulawitsi cried. "Look upon the shape formed by Grandfather of Gods —a shape never seen before."

Sayatasha, the Rain God of the North with the misty rain clouding around his single long horn, spoke then to the insect. "Why do you come, Our Grandfather? And what message do you bring to the Council of the Gods?"

"I come, oh Beloved Beings of the Sun-Father, to ask that you place your blessing upon two poor children: they who gave me this form and permission to be their messenger."

The Cornstalk Being then told how the boy of Ha'wi-k'uh was keeping life in the body of his sister and how, if their paths were to be fulfilled, they must have seed food to survive the winter.

The Council listened and when the insect had finished speaking, Sayatasha spoke:

"Sit happy, Our Grandfather, and we will instruct you what must be done, for we will happily help our beloved children at Ha'wi-k'uh." And Sayatasha showed the insect how the boy should cut prayer plumes and how they should be decorated with paint and with feathers, and how they should be offered, that the Council of the Gods might bring its blessings upon the children. And then Sayatasha summoned the He'hea-kwe, the Runners-of-the-Sacred-Dance, and instructed them to take corn grains and place them at Ha'wi-k'uh where Grandfather Insect would easily find them, so that the children would be fed while they were taught their duties. "Fly away now, Our Grandfather, to our beloved children, and instruct them well that they may have great blessings. Go happy!"

"Sit happy," said the Cornstalk Insect. With his wings buzzing, he darted upward through the watery roof and in a moment was flashing over the rooftops of Ha'wi-k'uh. Just as he flew down the smoke hole into the great room where the children were sleeping, he saw through the window of the upper room that the Runners-of-the-Sacred-Dance had already deposited hundreds of piles of yellow corn grains there.

The insect began darting back and forth, dropping corn kernels from the piles through a crack in the ceiling over the sleeping robes of the boy-child. *"Clunk, clunk, clunk, clunk, click,"* the kernels fell on the buffalo robe. Soon the robe was yellow with corn. The sound brought the boy part way out of the cave of sleep, enough to hear the sound and think in his doze that it was made by raindrops dripping, enough to feel the weight and think that his robe was growing with the weight of soaking dampness. He huddled under the robe, dreading the dawn when he would have to rise with everything cold and wet.

40

But when morning came and the boy pushed the robe back from his head, he shouted with delight. As he rose, hundreds of corn kernels poured down upon the floor in a golden flood. As he saw this, he thought of his Cornstalk Being and remembered releasing it the night before. But now it hung in its cage, just as it had since he had placed it there, without sound and without motion.

That morning the children were so happy they forgot, for the first time, that they had been left alone. They toasted some of the corn among the hot coals of the fireplace. Some they ground on the millstone into meal and this they cooked into

mush. Some they boiled with the poor bodies of the birds the boy had trapped. For the first time that winter, they were satisfied and their bellies were warm with food. All the long day they feasted, eating a little at a time, and as they ate they would raise their hands in blessing toward the insect—who simply hung there as if he were nothing but dead winter stalks.

When night came, and shadows danced around the room in the light from the fire, and the boy and his sister were full from feasting, the insect began to swing, ever so slowly, back and forth in his tiny cornstalk cage.

At first the boy was not sure. He had watched the insect all day long, and his sister had watched, but there had been no movement. Now the insect was swinging back and forth, and soon he began to speak.

"*Thli-ni-ni*," said the insect in his low humming whisper. "Let me go, for now I must teach you to make prayer plumes for the Council of the Gods."

The boy did not understand these things, for the old ones had left without instructing him. But the insect was now his friend, and he let him out of the cage.

No sooner was the door to the cage unfastened

than the insect darted out and circled around the room in the red glow from the firelight. He flew around the room three times, for his wings were stiff from sitting in the cage all day. Then he flew down next to the boy's ear.

"Have you feathers from the summer birds?" asked the insect. His voice was like the whisper of the wind in summer grasses.

Little sister, full from the day's feasting, had dropped off to sleep near the fire.

"Yes," said the boy. "Once, when I looked in the next room for paint, I found the feather box of my old ones. There were feathers from the duck and from the eagle."

"It is good," said the insect. "In the morning, when Sun-Father first smiles across the rooftops and the paths are still white with frost, go and cut sticks by the springs in the valley and bring them here. Choose plumes from the duck and from the eagle, and tie them to six sticks. The sticks must then be painted yellow, blue or green, red, white, speckled, and black. Do these things, that spring, which is the planting time, might be blessed with the breath of good fortune for you and your little sister."

"I will do as you have told me," said the boy, "but I may not do well. My father and my uncle, who made the prayer plumes, never told me of the way it should be done."

"You will do well," said the Cornstalk Insect. "And when you have finished I will take the plumes to the Council of the Gods, who shape the rain clouds in summer, and to the ancient ones."

Then the insect was finished talking, and the only sounds were the crackling of the fire, and the whirring of his wings as he flew out the sky hole into the night.

The boy sat very still in the glow from the fire and wondered where the Cornstalk Creature could have gone, but he was tired and soon he was fast asleep beside his sister.

When the room grew still and dark, and the embers from the fire were only a faint glow, and the stars were tiny points of light through the sky hole, the insect began his nightly work.

All night long the insect flew back and forth, dropping corn through the crack in the ceiling. When morning came, and Sun-Father climbed up over the mountains in the east and made the rooftops pink, there was the buffalo robe covered with golden grains of corn.

When the boy awoke, he saw the corn spread like a golden blanket over the buffalo robe.

"Thank you, My Father," he said to the Cornstalk Creature sitting motionless in its cage. "Thank you for dropping the corn in the night, and thank you for being so gentle and good to my little sister," he said. But the Cornstalk Being did not move.

After the boy had gathered the corn into a tray, and parched some for his little sister's breakfast, he set out along the path to the valley where the willow trees grew in clumps beside a spring. Sun-Father was not yet very high above the mountains, and the dead grass along the path was white with frost.

The boy selected only the straightest and best of the willow boughs, and when he had cut enough he tied them in a bundle and carried them home. He sat beside his sister near the fire. When he was warm he cut the willow boughs into wands. These he rubbed against pieces of sandstone until they were smooth.

Then, as the insect had directed, he tied the feathers on the ends of the sticks with brightly colored yarn from an old cotton kilt. When the feathers were tied securely, he painted the sticks. He painted them in the colors the insect had said, and when it was finished he tied the sticks together in a bundle and began to pray over them as he had seen his old ones do. The boy did not know the prayers of the ancients, so instead he made up his own prayer. Then he made an offering of prayer dust and sacred paint and laid it by in a corn shuck.

All day long the boy worked on the plumes and the prayer and the offering of sacred dust, and all day long the insect sat in his cornstalk cage and did not move. Sun-Father was just ending his journey across the wide sky when the boy finished his tasks.

Soon night settled like a dark blanket over the empty houses of the old ones. Darkness crept into the doorways and windows and filled the silent rooms, and the only light was a glow from the children's hearth.

The glow warmed the room and the children's faces, and once in a while the fire would flare up in the hearth and send shadows dancing across the walls and in and out of the corners, and then the Cornstalk Being began to stir.

He rocked back and forth for a moment in the firelight, then flicked out of his cage and out into the room. He flew three times around the room, then *flick*, he darted down and picked up the prayer plumes. *Flick*, he was gone out the smoke hole and into the starry night.

The little boy and his sister wondered where the Cornstalk Creature had gone, but he was their friend, whom they trusted, and they were not afraid. They curled up warm and snug under the buffalo robe, and by the time the fire had died down to a faint red glow in the hearth, they were asleep.

Again the Cornstalk Being circled high over the rooftops of Ha'wi-k'uh. He soared higher than the hunting eagle, higher even than the night wind, and then he shot westward like an arrow.

Over the great mesa he flew, and over the dark canyons and arroyos, until once again he hovered over the great blue lake with lights as numberless as winter stars.

Then down he dove, into the cold, clear water, and when he looked around he saw the Dance Hall of the Dead.

At the feet of Shulawitsi, the Little Fire God, the insect laid the sacred bundle of prayer plumes.

Shulawitsi waved his torch in the air until it burst into flames, and lit the Hall of the Dead. He looked upon the plumes of the eagle and the duck, and upon the brightly painted sticks, all just the right length and rubbed smooth with sandstone, and he was pleased.

"The youth whose hand has made these plumes shall become great in the eyes of his people," said Shulawitsi. "We have heard his prayers."

"*Ha'tchi, ha'tchi!*" said Pa'u-ti-wa, God of All Dance Gods, and the others all answered "*Ha'tchi,*" which meant that the Fire God had spoken well and true.

Then the Little Fire God spoke again to the insect.

"Return to the children and cherish them," he said. "When springtime comes to the valley of Ha'wi-k'uh, and it is once again planting time, we will shape the rain clouds high and wide and white above the mesas. Our swift runners will plant the flatlands from the seed stores of the gods."

This made the insect very happy. He flew from pot lip to blanket pole and hummed to himself.

Again the Fire God spoke.

"Do not fear for the little ones," he said to the Cornstalk Creature. "They shall complete their paths and be valuable to their people for generations, and generations after that."

Now this made the insect so happy that he could not sit still any longer. He flew up into the air, and he flew around the room three times. And then he flew down and hovered, on his tiny wings of cornstalk, near the Fire God's ear.

"I thank you for myself," he said, "and for my children who are very good." The creature's voice was just a whisper, for he was very small.

When he had given thanks, he darted up through the silent blue lake, up, higher than hunting eagles fly, up to where the sky begins. Then he turned toward the east and the faint yellow glow from Sun-Father where he rested behind the mountains.

When the children awoke the next morning, there sat the insect, still as cornstalk in his tiny cage.

4

Now as day followed day in that time just before spring, it happened that the little girl began to grow sick. She mourned often for her mother and her father, and her uncle, and nothing her brother could say made her feel better.

"You should not mourn for the old ones who left us to die from hunger and cold," he said, but still she would not be comforted.

When the fire had died away, and night had filled the room, and the little girl had finally cried herself to sleep, the Cornstalk Being slipped out of his cage and flew away through the smoke hole.

In the morning both the children were saddened, for the corn was almost gone from the storeroom, and worse than that, the cornstalk cage hung empty and very, very still.

The Cornstalk Being flew south over many mountains and across many plains. He flew as straight as a strained bow cord to the Land of Everlasting Summer. Everywhere there were birds and butterflies, and flowers of every color filled the air with their fragrance, and fruits hung ripe and heavy on all the trees.

In this valley the Corn Maidens lived. As the Cornstalk Being neared their home he rested, for his flight had stretched over many mountains and across many plains, and he was very tired.

Wherever a corn plant grew he rested on its tassels for a moment before flying on to the next one. In this way he flew and rested until he reached the home of the Corn Maidens.

The two sister maidens, who had dwelt for a time in the Cave of the White Cliffs, were strolling through the great fields of corn when they heard the insect. He made a sound like dry cornstalks in a summer wind.

"Hurry, sister," said the elder one. "Didn't you hear our child who comes from the Northland?"

"Where are you, oh child who art flesh of the corn plant?" she said.

"*Tsi-ni-thla*," buzzed the Cornstalk Being. "Here I am."

So the Corn Maidens looked and there he was, perched on a corn tassel, telling them of the children and their plight.

"We will hurry to them," said the elder sister, "for did they not once offer us food, thinking we were but poor beggars?"

"It is so," said the other sister. "We will not forget their goodness."

"Go before and tell our little son to prepare the corn rooms for us," said the elder sister. "For we will come to visit, and with us will come warm rains which will drive the cold snows away and bring the springtime."

Long before daylight the Cornstalk Being buzzed into the house of the children. He flew round and round the room, and then he flew round the boy's head until the boy awoke.

The room was still dark, for the fire had died away in the night, and Sun-Father had not yet crept up behind the mountains to the east. The boy sat up and listened to the buzzing of the Cornstalk Being, and rubbed his eyes, for he was still very sleepy.

"Wake up Little Father," said the Cornstalk Being, "for I have been to the Land of Everlasting Summer and talked to the Corn Maidens, and there is much that you should hear."

The boy's eyes became accustomed to the dark, and in the faint starlight through the smoke hole he could just make out the Cornstalk Being perched on the lip of a pot.

"I am awake," he whispered, for he did not want to wake his little sister.

"In the morning, when the light from Sun-Father fills the room, and your little sister wakes and begins to cry," whispered the Cornstalk Being in his tiny voice, "tell her that on the night of the third day her mothers, the Corn Maidens, are coming. You will know when it is their time, for a south wind will blow heavy with the scent of flowers and springtime, and a mist will melt away the frost of Sun-i-a-shi'wa-ni's breath. Then must you tell her to sleep, and before that night of the third day has passed the Corn Maiden Mothers will come into the room as softly as moonlight.

"Tomorrow and the next day you must clean out the corn rooms, for that is where the Corn Maidens will wish to stay, and when you have seen them you can take your little sister to them and she will be comforted."

When the Cornstalk Being had said all this, he flew to his perch in the tiny cage of grass straws and corn pith, and sat very still.

After that the little boy could not sleep, and just before daybreak he arose and kindled a fire in the hearth. By the light of the fire he began cleaning the great room in which he and his sister lived. Then when Sun-Father rose over the eastward mountains and painted the rooftops red, the boy began cleaning the empty corn rooms.

When his little sister awoke, the boy ran to where she lay under the buffalo robe.

"See, little sister," he said, "I am cleaning the house, for our mothers are coming." But the little girl thought he was only trying to comfort her and she cried anyway.

All day long the little boy cleaned the corn rooms, and all the next day, for he was weak, and it took a long time to clean all the dust and cobwebs away with a little hand-broom made of straw.

Finally, all the rooms were finished, and in each room the boy spread old blankets and soft things, so that the Corn Maidens would be pleased and would not leave his little sister.

On the third day the little sister cried more than she ever had before, because for two days her brother had told her the Corn Maiden Mothers were coming. So the little boy kept climbing the ladder and looking out the smoke hole to see if the rain clouds were building.

At last, far away to the south, he saw clouds of mist gather and rise high above the mesa, and in his face blew a soft breeze that smelled of flowers and springtime.

"They are coming, little sister," he shouted as he climbed down the ladder. "They are coming. Soon, the Corn Maidens will be here to comfort you."

Sun-Father moved behind the clouds, and the rain began to fall, and the Cornstalk Creature began to buzz joyfully around the room.

It was dim, for Sun-Father was still behind the clouds, but the light from the smoke hole poured in and filled the room. Then, right before the little boy's eyes, the form of a beautiful maiden floated down the ladder and past him into the corn room, and behind the first Corn Maiden, a second.

Then from the corn room came a voice as soft as bird song.

"Come, Little-Boy-Who-Comforts-His-Sister," said the voice, "that you might be comforted."

So the little boy went into the corn room where he had cleaned and spread the blankets and soft things, and there stood the Maiden Mothers of Corn who were the gentlest and loveliest beings the boy had ever seen. He forgot they were not his own mother, and he ran up to where they stood. They knelt down and took him in their arms and kissed him and stroked his cheeks, and it all made him very, very happy, for even though he had been strong and had taken care of his little sister, he was still just a little boy.

Then he carried his sleeping sister into the presence of the Maidens, where he laid her on a soft blanket. He kindled a flame on the hearth of the empty room. The fire leaped and danced in the hearth and made the room cheerful and warm. The Corn Maidens sang to the little ones, and while they sang the Cornstalk Creature hummed down from his cage and settled in the doorway. Finally the little girl opened her sunken eyes and smiled about.

"See," said the little boy, "I told you the Mothers of Corn were coming. It is as the Cornstalk Creature told me, in the night."

For as long as the firelight lasted the Maiden Mothers of Corn soothed and comforted the children. They stroked their hair and cradled them in their arms and sang soft slow songs until the children fell into a deep slumber.

When the children were sound asleep, and the fire had died down very low, the Corn Maidens drew from the folds of their robes many wonderful things. An ear each of yellow, red, blue, white, and speckled corn, they laid carefully on the floor of the corn room. Over the ears of corn they placed little embroidered sashes of cotton, and on the blanket poles they hung beads of shell and turquoise, and many bright garments.

All these things were but the seeds of all the wonderful things which the Mothers of Seed knew best how to multiply, as the corn, which is really their flesh, multiplies itself many times from a single grain.

The house where the children's uncle had lived was large, and in all the many rooms the Corn

Maidens placed baskets of green corn, and fruits, and melons, and gourds, and all manner of good things, and all of the things were but seeds of things to come. Then the Maidens went to where the children lay sleeping, and they saw that the children had changed. The little girl was fair and bright and her hair was soft, and the pallor of winter was lifted; and the boy, who was only a child, looked stronger and older, and his face shone with kindness and his bearing was of one much beloved by his people.

When the Maiden Mothers saw that it was good with the children they glided softly out of the house and down the hill to the home of the aged grandmother.

They called in at the doorway and a startled voice bade them enter. When the old woman saw who it was, she covered her face with her hands and knelt at their feet.

"You are a good old mother," said the White Corn Maiden, "and that is why we have come to ask your help."

And then the Maiden told the old woman how the children had been left alone when the village was emptied, and how—from the flesh of the corn plant—a being was made to watch over the children, and how the children and the Cornstalk

Being lived in a house across the village and over the hill from the old woman's house.

"Go to comfort the little girl, for she is but a baby," said the Yellow Corn Maiden, "and be as a mother to her, for she shall become the mother of her people, and her children shall be mothers of the people. Go also and look after the little boy, for when the corn grows tall and green in the valley, and the tassels ripen and turn yellow in the sun, he shall become the father of his people."

Then the White Corn Maiden said to the old woman, "But not until the Cornstalk Being has gone away shall you abide with the little ones. Be content to dwell in your poor house, and when you are needed the Being will summon you."

The Corn Maidens then blessed the old woman, who was no longer poor and ugly, but a kind, fair old mother, with long beautiful strands of white hair, and quickly they returned to the house of the little ones. There, they spoke to the boy of the many things which were soon to pass. Soon, they said, the boy's oldest uncle would return for a loom which was lying in one corner of the house, for now the uncle and his people had to weave and work for the Hopis for their food.

"Our warm rains melted the snow on the trail," said the White Corn Maiden, "and even now your

61

oldest uncle prepares for his journey. On the eighth morning he will enter this, the old home of his people. He will see the smoke rising from your smoke hole, and he will come tired but eager at your ladder.

"He will greet you and your sister with joy, but you must neither speak to him, nor accept the food he offers. Not until the fourth day will you speak to him. By then he will have been puzzled by your silence, and have pondered its meanings, and will have guessed in the wisdom of his years that you have last spoken to the Beloved Ones. He will forget that you are but a stripling, not yet initiated into your clan. When you speak, he will be humble before you, and wonder at your wisdom, and he will bow to you and become your faithful servant.

"When all this is done, you shall declare him a warrior-priest, and bid him return to the nation of the Hopis and gather our people once again to relight the hearth fires of Ha'wi·k'uh and replant the wasted fields of the Valley of the Hot Waters."

This made the little boy very happy, for he and his sister were saddened when they saw the empty rooms where their people had once lived. It would be a good thing, he thought, for the rooms to hear laughter again, and to have the smoke make blue lines into the morning sky above Ha'wi·k'uh.

Then the Yellow Corn Maiden spoke to the boy.

"Should your little sister cry for us," she said, "have the Cornstalk Being bring the grandmother, who, like you, was left when the people went to live far away.

"Be as good as you have been," she cautioned, "and you will grow wise and powerful. Keep your heart good and gentle, and counsel the bad among your people as a father counsels the foolish among his children. If you do these things, then this valley will be blessed with our presence, and the corn will multiply, and the squash, and all the food of the people, and the land of the people will be filled with plenty."

Then each of the Corn Maidens in turn took the boy's face and breathed upon his forehead, and then they said, "May each day bring you happiness, and as much happiness as the day has brought, so much may the evening bring."

"Go now in with your little sister," said the elder maiden, "for we depart and you will see us no more, save with the eyes of your dreams."

As daylight broke in the east behind the mountain, the Corn Maidens faded from sight, and their voices faded away to bird songs.

When the Corn Maidens had departed the boy went softly to his sister. All around her were baskets of fragrant fruits and melons, and in the corn rooms were piles and baskets of the golden grain.

"Feast happily on that brought by the Corn Maidens," he said to her, and she feasted on melons and on the corn that he had parched. And when they had eaten their fill the boy cast the leavings outside to the birds and the rodents.

Then it happened that one morning the little girl felt sad, but she did not cry and did not tell her brother. The Cornstalk Being knew that she was sad, and he fluttered and buzzed about until he sang himself right out the window. After a few moments he returned, and close behind him followed the old woman who lived alone below the hill.

She was dressed exactly as the Corn Maidens had been, and when the little girl saw her she ran up and buried her face in the folds of the old woman's white robe. The old woman bounced the little girl on her knee and told her such pretty tales of the old times that the little girl had to laugh, in spite of herself.

When the old woman left she told the little girl she would come again from time to time to see her and her little brother, and when the little girl heard this she was so happy she laughed out loud, and her laughter was like the brook tumbling down over smooth rocks at the head of the valley. It was a springtime sound, made of melting snow.

5

Soon after the old woman's visit, it was time for the arrival of the uncle. The boy carefully cleared away all traces of food from the sitting place in the house, and he put away all the garments brought by the Corn Maidens. Then he built a great fire in the hearth, so that the smoke might rise high above the village of Ha'wi-k'uh. Then they heard the uncle's footsteps on the pathway outside, and his weary feet upon the ladder and his steps upon the roof. And then his old eyes were looking through the sky hole into the room where the children were sitting. He saw them and he was amazed and overjoyed. "Ah, my beloved little ones," he said. "Is it possible? Is it possible that I see you again after all these many days?"

To his surprise the children neither smiled nor spoke to him. They seemed not to notice his presence.

"My beloved little ones," he said as he bent over them until his gray hairs almost touched their faces, "don't you know that I am your old uncle?"

Still nothing. The little children neither smiled nor spoke.

The uncle stood up sorrowfully and looked around the room. It was as bare as when the people had left for the Hopi villages. The only difference was that now it was clean and well-ordered. Of food or clothing or the utensils of daily living there was no trace.

"Poor little creatures," the uncle thought to himself. "I will offer them food, for it may be that they have lived as prairie dogs live in winter— sound asleep."

He unwrapped his burden and mixed a gruel of ground corn and water. This he placed before the little ones, and said, "Eat all you can, my children, for it has been a long winter, and very cold."

Still the children neither spoke nor smiled nor seemed in any way to notice his presence.

The uncle grew fearful, and moved away from the children and closer to the hearth.

"They are not living," he thought to himself, "but the Beloved Ones whose paths have been completed." But while he looked at them so fresh and strong with their cheeks full of color he knew it was not so. "Besides," he thought again, "if they were truly returned from the Dance Hall of the Dead, I would see them only in the night."

"My little ones," he said aloud again, "your mother and father and all the brothers and sisters of your clan are well, and may soon come back to live at Ha'wi-k'uh. My joy is great at seeing you unharmed, and theirs will be yet greater. Will you not also be glad to see them?"

And still the children made no answer, but sat very still and gazed upon the fire.

Once again the uncle cast his eyes about the room. Then he took the bundle from his back and hung it on one of the steps of the ladder. From the bundle he took flour and dried meat dust and hastily made a meal, but before sitting down to eat he asked the children again to share his food. Still there was no reply.

The old uncle ate a few mouthfuls in silence, but he felt so sad about the children that the tears began to stream down the side of his face. The boy was filled with compassion for the old uncle, but he remembered the instructions given by the Corn Maidens and he said not a word.

At last the old uncle finished his meal, and after he had placed the remaining morsels carefully away he turned again toward the little boy.

"I cannot remain here long. My provisions are scant and the journey back to our people is long and hard, but I will stay for three or four days and gather wood for your fire. I will do this so that when the night settles like a blanket over the empty houses, you and your little sister will be warm, and your room will be lighted against the night shadows."

At this the little boy bowed his head and smiled, and the old uncle was greatly relieved to see some sign of life.

As soon as the uncle went for firewood, the little boy brought out melons and green corn, which the Maidens had provided. When the children had eaten their fill, they cleaned away all traces of the food.

It happened thus, until the fourth day when the uncle went as usual for wood. He had scarcely been gone a minute when the old woman of the broken house came in and helped the children prepare a great feast and spread it on one of the embroidered mantles left by the Maidens of Corn.

There were melons of green and red, and yellow squash, and beans, and mountains of golden corn, and cakes of meal, and all manner of fruit from trees along the river, and all manner of food from the seed left by the Maidens of Corn.

When the baskets were filled to overflowing with the food, and the air in the room was full and heavy with the smell of fruit, and the feast was in readiness, then the children dressed themselves in the splendid embroideries and ornaments left by the Corn Maidens.

Scarcely were all the preparations complete when the uncle suddenly appeared at the sky hole. As he descended the ladder with his burden of firewood, the uncle's eyes fell upon the old woman, whom he addressed as "Mother," in the way one greets a superior and beloved being, and he breathed upon her hands to show his respect for her.

Then he looked upon the little boy and his sister with wonder and, being wise and heavy with many years, he knew that they had been somehow touched by A'wonawil'ona—the Creator and Container of All—and he breathed upon their hands also.

"Sit with us, Uncle, and eat, for we know you are very hungry," said the little boy. "You brought few provisions, which you offered freely, and you have gathered wood for our fire, now it is four days."

And saying that, the boy took first from each of the vessels and baskets of food a morsel of each kind. Then he cast them into the fire saying, "Makers of the trails of our lives and ye spirits of our ancestors, of this add ye unto your hearts after the manner of your own knowledge, and bless us with fruitful seasons, needed water, and age of life."

They ate of all the food spread before them, the uncle with a trembling hand for he was indeed hungry, and the boy sparingly and with great deliberation, in the manner most becoming to a wise and great person.

When they were finished, the old woman and the little sister cleared away the remnants and laid them away for the seed-eaters outside. Then the boy spoke to the uncle.

"Uncle and child, come and sit close to me," he said, "for there is much that I must say and you must hear."

The uncle moved nearer the boy. "What is it, My Father?" he said, for now he knew that the boy was endowed with the spirit of a wise priest and a father's commanding.

And then the little boy, who had been made wise, began to speak, and as he spoke he looked into the fire.

"You and your people, alas, alas!" he said. "Not only did they make sport of the blessings of the Beloved, but even of the Beloved themselves. Of myself and my little sister, their own flesh and blood, they thought not, but left us to perish. Sad were the ways of the people after that, and it was a teaching that they might be wiser in the future."

"It is indeed as you have said, My Father," said the uncle. He sat with his arms wrapped around his knees, and he knew that what the boy said was true.

"Those who were our parents," said the boy, "behold, they shall henceforth be our children, and their offspring shall be the servants of our off-spring."

And then the boy looked straight at the uncle and said, "Yet I remember you did not join in the folly of the others. You alone warned against it. Therefore you alone shall enjoy my best favor. You are wise, and long will you serve as my war-rior-priest."

Then the boy spoke of the old woman, whom the people of Ha'wi-k'uh had despised.

"No longer shall she be despised," said the wise boy. "No longer shall she rummage among the leavings of the town for her food, and no longer shall she live alone in her broken house below the hill, for she shall be the mother of her people until the end of her days. And when that time comes, then shall the little sister become the Mother of Seed, for she has tasted the milk of the Corn Maidens."

Then the boy spoke of the people.

"No longer may the people live according to their own wills," he said, "but rather as children, whom a father and his brother must guide, counsel, and command. I am their father for I have tasted of the flesh of the Corn Maidens and thus it will be until the days of our people are spent."

"Four days you shall spend here to rest yourself," the boy said to the uncle. "Then you shall return to the country of the Hopis and summon my people."

As evening came it grew dark earlier than usual, and the clouds boiled and churned high above the mesas, and then the thunder came with a great crashing and rumbling, and the lightning cracked and snapped about the buttes and lit the darkness under the clouds with hard blue flashes, and the smell of rain was in the air.

It fell in torrents over the parched land. It fell on the mountains high above the village and it fell over the mesas and in the valley where the stream

tumbled over the round rocks and boulders. The water foamed down off the mesas and boiled through the arroyos until, finally, it spread out in ever-widening fans across the floor of the valley and laid down a fertile layer of fresh new soil.

Then, as the moon rose over the Zuni buttes, there came, silent as hawks, many runners from the Dance of the Gods in the Lake of the Dead, and with them came many strong warriors. Into the rich new soil they planted, everywhere, corn of all kinds and food seeds from the storehouses of the gods. And then once again, in the quiet time before dawn, the rain came.

It came soft as rabbit skin and it touched the mounds of earth covering the many-colored kernels of seed corn, and when the rain had gone the breath of the Corn Maidens fanned the country with warmth from the Land of Everlasting Summer.

When Sun-Father moved from his lodge behind the eastern mountains and flooded the valley with orange light, not a footprint could be seen in all the great plain. Yet everywhere there were rows of yellow and green corn plants and melon vines, shooting forth from the warm soil.

Light crept into the house on long yellow shafts, and after everyone was awake and had eaten the morning meal, the boy called to his uncle.

"Come with me, my warrior-priest," he said, and together they climbed the ladders to the highest part of the house.

"Behold," said the boy as he pointed to the field of sprouting corn. "Behold the planting of the Beloved!"

"You will go now, my warrior," said the boy. "Take with you now such provisions as you will need for the journey to our people. Take also a plant of corn as a promise of harvest to the A'shiwi, for they have forgotten by now the sound of truth. Before you have reached the land of the Hopis, this corn plant shall have grown milky and full of kernel, and it shall be your proof."

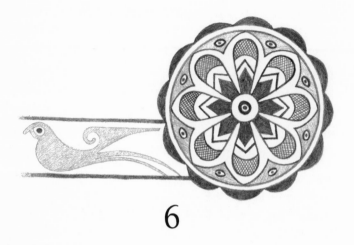

6

Now as it happened, the Cornstalk Being had kept as still and quiet as if he were only corn pith and straw while the uncle stayed with the boy and his sister. But on the night after the uncle had departed, the tiny creature once again began to rock nervously back and forth on his perch, impatient for the night to end. Toward daylight he could not sit still a minute more, and softly he called to the boy.

"Father of His People, hear me now," buzzed the creature, but soft enough not to wake the little sister.

"Father of His People, hear me now," he buzzed again, and this time the boy awoke and slipped quietly out from under the buffalo robe.

"I hear you, My-Friend-Who-Art-Made-of-Corn," said the boy, "but the fire is gone and Sun-Father has not yet come, and I cannot see you in the dark."

"It is of no importance," said the creature. "It is almost time for me to go, yet there are things which must pass between us. Of these things I now speak," and then the creature buzzed down close to the boy's ear in the dark, so that the little sister would not awaken.

"You have given me life," said the creature, "even as I and the Mothers of Corn have given you new life."

"It is so," said the boy.

"Precious shall you be," said the creature, "and your people shall plant and reap for you and your chosen council of wise ones. And when you have fulfilled your path and joined the everlasting Council of the Dead, the offspring of your flesh or breath shall be as precious to the people as you have been.

"By my ministry," the creature continued, "and from the milk of the Mother Maidens of Seed you have received being as both a man and shi-wa-ni,

77

which means priest, and your little sister shall be the Seed Priestess of Earth, keeper of seed among men, and provider of the fertility of the seeds whereby men live."

"It will be as it will be," said the boy, for he was wise now beyond his years and knew of the responsibility that had been given him.

While they talked, light began to creep into the east, and from behind the mountains which were still black there came a soft blue glow from Sun-Father's first awakening. In the light that was not yet light the boy could barely make out the blur from the creature's cornstalk wings, as he hovered silently in the still room.

"Behold," said the creature. "It is almost time, yet there is a final thing."

"I will hear it," said the boy.

And then the creature told how it was that he was born of the flesh of the Mother Maidens of both men and creatures.

"In my being their flesh is renewed," said the tiny creature, "and amidst the corn tassels shall I find my home. Yet it was to be your messenger that I was made, therefore never very long in any of my many homes shall I rest."

And then he said to the boy, "Make another of my form from the cornstalks growing now in the fields below, and send her forth, and men shall call us and our offspring 'Dragonflies'."

And that is how it is that there are Dragonflies.

"It will be done," said the boy. "In remembrance of your faithful service I will paint your form on sacred things as a symbol of the god-given rains of springtime, and your companion shall be painted as the symbol of summer and the pools of summer showers."

When eight days had passed, over the north-western hills came the nation of Ha'wi-k'uh, and with them came many strangers from other tribes and countries. When they entered the town through vast fields of ripening corn they passed beneath the house of the great priest-boy, and breathed with humility their spirits upon his hands.

From among the strangers who came that day, the young priest chose three. These three he embraced and called younger brothers, and into them he breathed the breath which had been breathed into him by the Mothers of Corn.

Then he chose a great warrior and placed him under the old uncle, and gave them command of the nation.

When he had done this he spoke to the two warrior-priests.

"Go now," he said to them, "and command the people in the harvest of the gods. Each man shall take seven loads of corn for himself, but the eighth load shall he take for my brothers and me, that all the people shall keep respect for our counsel in their hearts."

When the corn was gathered, the boy who was now a great priest had many storerooms filled. This

he saved, that it might furnish seed for the people,
or food in time of want. Portions of the stored
harvest he gave to the Beloved Ones, the ancestral
spirits, and the seed-eaters that they might be content and not raid the corn bins at night.

By and by it was that the boy-priest grew great
in the eyes of his people, and when several years
had passed he married the most beautiful of mai-

dens, and his daughters when they had grown were sought for their beauty and radiance by men from all towns both far and near.

This is how it was in the days of the ancients very long ago, and that is how there came to be the Ta'a'shi-wa-ni, or Corn Priests of Zuni.

Author's Notes on
The Boy Who Made Dragonfly

Its Form: In our society, the account of the boy who made the first dragonfly would be called a "Bible story." Like stories based on the Old Testament or Pentateuch, this narrative is intended to teach both the history and morality of a people. There is one important difference. The Zunis had no written language to keep alive their tribal wisdom. Instead it was passed on orally—memorized by children who, in turn, taught it to their own children.

This particular story was first recorded in writing in 1883. Frank Hamilton Cushing, a young Easterner, came to the Zuni Pueblo in 1879 to study the tribe for the Bureau of American Ethnology. Strongly attracted to the Zunis, Cushing abandoned his white man's ways and was accepted as a member of the tribe. He was initiated into the Macaw Clan and, before his death, had become the Chief Priest of the Bow Society—one of the most "valuable men" in Zuni tribal life.

Its Place: In terms of "mythic time" this story seems to have come relatively late in the development of the

Zuni culture. The Zuni clans had almost completed their legendary wanderings in search of the Middle Place of the World, where they were destined to live. In fact, Ha'wi·k'uh was the next-to-last stop for these previously migratory people. When they abandoned this village for good, in about 1672, it was to move a few miles northward to the present site of the Zuni Pueblo. Their legend tells us that the Water Strider, a mythic being, helped the Zunis in their search. He stretched his many legs to the edges of the earth and lowered his body. The point where it touched the earth (a low hill beside the Zuni river, south of Gallup, New Mexico) was It'a-wa-na (The Middle Place) and there the Zunis built the stone-and-adobe Zuni Pueblo which they call Halona It'a-wa-na (Ant Hill of the Middle Place). This, legend tells us, is to be their home until time ends for the Zunis.

In terms of "historic time" this story was probably first told more than five hundred, and less than six hundred, years ago. We know that Ha'wi·k'uh was founded about seven hundred years ago, about the year 1300. The story seems to be based on a drought-famine which happened after this village had time to become a well-established community, but before the arrival of the first European explorers (1539–1540) began disrupting the patterns of Indian civilizations.

Zuni Mythology: In the beginning, the Zuni version of the Old Testament Genesis tells us there was only a formless mist and *A'wonawil'ona*, who is the Great God and Container of All Things. *A'wonawil'ona* created the Sun-Father, and the Moon, and two super-human beings, whom the Zunis call *Shi-wa-ni* and *Shi-wa-no-kia*. These two created the starry skies and the earth, and deep within the earth they produced living beings that were to become men and other animals and insects.

Zuni mythology tells how these beings, with help of two sons of the Sun, worked their way from the total darkness of the fourth underworld to the Water Moss World, and from there upward to the Mud World, and thence upward to the World of Wings, and finally, through the waters of a lake, to the surface of the earth. There, after losing their tails and other animal-like features, some of these beings became men. The Zuni clans then began their migrations in search of the Middle Place, obtained corn, learned to hunt, and founded the various religious societies and priest-hoods.

Zuni Attitudes: Much that might seem strange in the story of the dragonfly becomes clear, if one under-stands the basic Zuni religious philosophy. The story of creation in the Old Testament teaches us that we were made lords of the universe, with dominion over the birds and the beasts. The Zuni story of creation and emergence makes him one with the universe. He, as a man, is part of a universal harmony with the deer, the dung beetle, the spider, the bee, the cloud, the wind, the bear, and the cactus. Every part of nature is to be treated with respect. Thus, the offense of the

Zunis in wasting their food supplies (which showed disrespect for the plants and rain and earth which provided it) would seem more serious in their eyes than it might to us. The same can be said for the failure to feed the Corn Maidens in their disguise as ragged old women. In Zuni philosophy all humans are brothers, and strangers must be treated with great hospitality. The "prayer meal" mentioned in the story is, of course, finely ground corn meal, which the Zunis and many other Southwestern Indians use to this day in ceremonials, much as Catholics use "holy water" and some other religions use aromatic oils. In fact, in the Catholic church at Zuni, one finds corn meal in the holy-water font at the entrance. The philosophy behind its use is basic: corn represents the supreme blessing from God, allowing a wandering tribe of hunters and seed gatherers to put down roots, become farmers, and develop a civilization. Meal of corn thus symbolizes all blessings.

The Zuni practice of breathing upon another's hands combines the meanings we attach to shaking hands, hugging one another, and bowing. The gesture involves both respect and love—the breath coming, as it does, directly from the spirit within.

Since ties of family are unusually strong among Zunis (and most other Southwestern Indians), kinship titles are often used to denote respect and/or affection. Thus, the effigy of the dragonfly is called "Grandfather" in recognition of his wisdom.

Format by Joyce Hopkins
Set in 12pt. Baskerville
Composed by The Haddon Craftsmen, Inc.
Printed by The Murray Printing Company
Bound by The Haddon Craftsmen, Inc.
HARPER & ROW PUBLISHERS, INCORPORATED